Whale Rescue

Sue Mongredien

Illustrated by Maria Pearson

USBORNE

First published in the UK in 2010 by Usborne Publishing Ltd., Usborne House,
83-85 Saffron Hill, London EC1N 8RT, England. www.usborne.com

A CIP catalogue record for this book is available from the British Library.

FMAMJJASOND/19

ISBN 9781409506393 02961-3

Printed in India

Contents

Shanti

Molly

Eloise

Leila

Undersea Kingdom

Queen
Luna

Aisha

Iona

Phoebe

Chapter One

It was a December afternoon and Molly was
writing Christmas cards to her friends.

To Katie, Happy Christmas, Love Molly

To Francesca, Happy Christmas, Love Molly

To Chloe, Happy Christmas, Love Molly...

"Do you want a mince pie, Molly? Gran and
I made them while you were at school, and
they're still warm."

Molly looked up at the sound of her mum's

voice. "Yes, please," she said, unable to resist the tantalizing smell of spicy fruit and pastry that was wafting through from the kitchen.

She sat up as her mum passed her a bowl filled with two mince pies and cream, and dug a spoon in hungrily. "Mmm," she said at the first mouthful. Now she felt *really* Christmassy!

She and her parents had decorated the house last night with sprays of holly, and strings of red and gold sparkly tinsel, and it looked so pretty. At school, they had been practising the

Christmas play every day, and had made all sorts of glitter-covered pictures and gifts to take home at the end of term. Molly always loved this time of year, and the parties and carol concerts and the fun things she'd been doing at school made it feel extra special.

Her eye fell on the pile of Christmas cards on the floor. That made her feel happy too – that she had so many friends to give cards to now. Molly's family had moved to Horseshoe Bay back in the summer and, at first, she'd missed her friends from her old school and had been rather lonely. Now she was much more settled in her new school, and was enjoying getting to know the girls in her class. And of course, ever since she'd become the Secret Mermaid she had her mermaid friends too… and the times she'd spent with them had been the most wonderful and exciting experiences of her life!

Gran made her way slowly into the living room just then, leaning on her stick, and put the television on before sinking into the sofa. "You've been busy," she commented, indicating the pile of cards. "I hope there's one for me there, too."

Molly smiled at her gran. "You get a special one," she told her, thinking about the snowflake cards she'd painted at school, one for each member of her family – even Toby, her baby brother. Gran deserved an especially nice present, Molly thought to herself. After all, it

had been Gran who'd given Molly her best gift ever – the magic shell necklace that took her into the mermaid world of the Undersea Kingdom, where Molly had had so many amazing adventures.

Gran was watching a news programme on the television, and Molly found herself half-listening as she finished her mince pies (delicious!) and went back to writing cards.

Dear Tess, Happy Christmas, Love—

But then her attention was caught by something the news reporter said, and Molly's pen almost skidded off the paper as she looked up at the screen.

"At this time of year, here on the Pacific

Coast of Mexico, you can usually see hundreds of grey whales arriving from their feeding grounds of Alaska, as part of their annual migration," the reporter was saying. He was standing on a deserted beach, gesturing at the empty blue sea behind him. "The whales migrate from the cooler waters where they feed in the summer months, to warmer waters, such as this part of the ocean, in winter months, to give birth to their young. But this year, their migration pattern seems to have changed," he went on, sounding concerned. "There's no sign of any whales here yet – and we've had similar reports from other migration hot spots around the world." He frowned into the camera, holding his hands wide. "The question is, where are all the whales – and what does this mean for their future?"

An icy chill went down Molly's back as she watched some old footage of whales joyfully leaping high out of the water – or breaching, as she had learned it was called. *She* knew  what had happened to the whales, of course. They had been captured by Carlotta, a bad mermaid, who called herself the Dark Queen.

Carlotta had not only imprisoned all the whales of the oceans, but she'd captured the dolphins, seahorses, turtles, penguins and octopuses too. Molly had been helping the Animal-Keeper mermaids track them down and set them free, but they still hadn't been able to find the whales and octopuses. And now that the rest of the world had noticed the whales had vanished, surely it wouldn't be long before people started looking into their disappearance a little closer, and asking questions.

Molly shivered at the thought. She knew she had to keep the mermaids' existence a secret – nobody must be allowed to find out about them! She knew, too, that she had to help her mermaid friends find the missing whales and octopuses as soon as possible.

"Everything all right, my love?" came Gran's voice just then, and Molly turned to see her grandmother looking quizzically at her.

Molly struggled to find the right words to reply. Gran had been "the secret mermaid" in her time, just as Molly was now, so she knew about Molly's underwater adventures. But the Merqueen herself, Queen Luna, had forbidden

Molly to talk to anyone, even Gran, about them. "Not really," Molly said honestly in the end. "But...I'm hoping it will be again soon."

Gran nodded, her eyes understanding. "I hope so too," she said.

That night, when Molly had said goodnight to her parents and Gran, and was tucked up in bed, she glanced over at the magical mermaid shell lying on her bedside table and had a prickling feeling of trepidation. She loved her mermaid adventures, but the last one, when she'd helped a mermaid called Shanti find and rescue the missing turtles, had been very scary. Each time Molly and the mermaids had found the imprisoned animals, they'd been attacked by a variety of monsters left there by the Dark Queen to guard the creatures. The monsters guarding the turtles had been the most aggressive yet, attacking Molly and Shanti with lumps of coral and stones.

Thankfully she'd been able to defeat the monsters every time so far with the magic powers of a special animal charm she had on her shell necklace, but it was always dangerous, and Molly couldn't help feeling frightened that the Dark Queen's power was increasing by the day. She was sure her luck couldn't hold out for ever.

Just as Molly was thinking this, she saw the familiar pink light stream from her mermaid shell into the darkness of her bedroom, and in the next instant, she felt the extraordinary magic beginning again. She shut her eyes as her whole body started to tingle, and then she felt as if she were falling very quickly from a great height. Exhilaration rushed through her at the sensation – it was like being on a roller coaster, or the fastest, steepest slide in the world. Her heart leaped excitedly but she felt nervous too. What would happen to her when she became a mermaid this time?

Chapter Two

Moments later, Molly felt cool water around her and opened her eyes to see that, yes, she'd transformed into a mermaid once again, with a gorgeous glittering tail in place of her legs! She was in a stretch of open sea, with rocks on the seabed below, and shoals of fish cruising past, their silvery bodies sparkling as they moved.

"Molly!" came a voice, and Molly turned eagerly to see Leila, one of the Animal-Keeper

mermaids, waving as she swam
towards her. Leila had beautiful
coffee-coloured skin, and long,
curly black hair which was pulled back
into a ponytail with a pink hairband that
matched her tail. She wore a bright orange
halter-neck top.

"Hi," Molly said, spotting the pretty whale charm that Leila wore on her necklace, and remembering that Leila was the mermaid responsible for looking after all the whales of the oceans. "How are things? Any sign of the whales?"

"Not yet, no," Leila said, "although I've got a strong sense that they might be somewhere near here. I met a couple of porpoises just now who looked really spooked. They said they could hear music when they swam past an old deserted shipwreck, but they couldn't see where the sound was coming from." A hopeful light shone in her brown eyes. "I can't help wondering if the music might have come from my whales."

"I hope so," Molly replied. She'd heard whalesong before and would never forget the sound of the graceful humpback whales singing their haunting, melodic tunes. "Where is this shipwreck? Let's check it out. Although..." She glanced around and lowered her voice, suddenly remembering the reef monsters she'd had to escape from last time. "We need to be careful," she said. "If the whales *are* nearby, the Dark Queen is sure to have posted some of her army to keep watch over them."

Leila nodded. "Shanti told me what happened," she said. "We'll have to be on our guard." She pointed into the distance. "The shipwreck is this way. Let's take a look."

They swam together for a few minutes, then a large, dark shape appeared some way in the distance. As they got closer, Molly realized that it was the wreckage of an old trawler boat, lying on its side on the seabed. There was a large hole in the boat's hull, as if it had been ripped open on a rock, and the sides of the boat were covered in barnacles, with seaweed and other sea plants growing around it.

"It's huge," Molly said as they drew closer to it. "I wonder where—"

She'd been about to say she wondered where the porpoises had heard the music, but she didn't need to finish her sentence. For suddenly, she and Leila heard the faint, high-pitched notes of whales singing too, and they stared at each other in excitement.

"It's them!" Leila exclaimed, her eyes huge with delight. "It's the whales!"

Quickly, the two mermaids made their way around the boat, trying to track the faint strains of music. Molly slid through the old iron door-frames and into wrecked cabins,

where sailors once must have snored in their
sleep, but which were now full of seawater.
Molly knew she had to examine every part of the
ship carefully. Carlotta had used some powerful
bad magic to make all the creatures a fraction of

their usual sizes in order to steal some of their life force, and then she'd imprisoned them in sealed spaces. The penguins had been trapped in an air bubble at the top of a huge iceberg, whereas the turtles had been shrunk to fit inside an egg. Where had Carlotta hidden the whales?

Molly pored over every piece of wood and metal, under every plant and stone, eager to spot a trace of them. As well as shrinking the animals to tiny sizes, Carlotta had also stolen their special abilities – the dolphins could no longer swim at their super speeds, and the sea horses could no longer camouflage themselves by changing colour.

None of the mermaids knew why the Dark Queen had done this, other than to make herself even more powerful. They were all wondering what she was plotting next – and dreading finding out...

"Where can they be?" Molly sighed, after she and Leila had been searching for a while. "Their music is so faint, it's really difficult to pinpoint exactly where it's coming from."

"Maybe they're not even *in* the boat," Leila replied, looking baffled.  "We've scoured every centimetre of it now and haven't seen so much as a tail. Maybe we should look in a slightly wider circle around here."

"Good idea," Molly agreed, and began to swim slowly around the base of the huge boat, looking out for anything unusual that might contain the missing whales. Then, as she neared a cluster of grey rocks, she noticed that the singing had become a little louder and she dived impulsively towards the rocks for a closer look.

The singing was definitely louder there, and it made Molly's skin prickle with excitement. She was near the whales now, she felt absolutely sure of it. Were they trapped in a rocky crevice, or—

"Ahh!" she murmured, spotting an old wicker lobster-trap half-hidden amid the boulders. She pulled it up and opened the lid to see that, yes, there were thousands of microscopic whales the size of small tadpoles inside it – but they were sealed beneath a glassy layer that she couldn't immediately break. "Leila!" Molly hissed delightedly. "I've found them!"

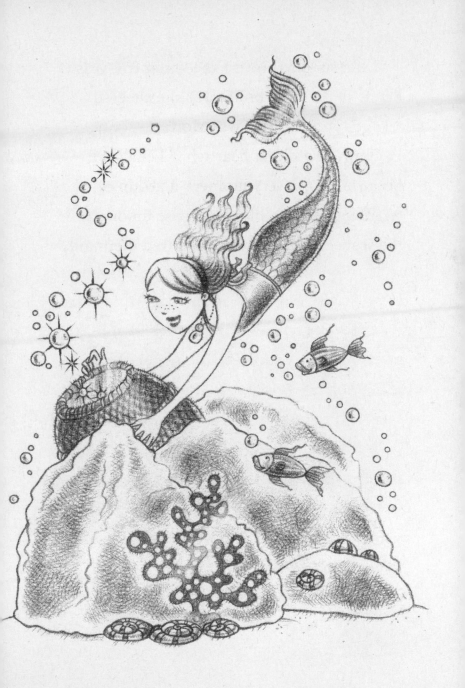

Leila surged through the water towards her at once. "Oh, brilliant!" she cheered. "That's wonderful news, Molly, I—"

But Molly didn't hear what Leila said, because at that very moment a group of terrifying-looking monsters rose up out of the seabed behind the dark-haired mermaid.

They were tall and menacing, and seemed to be made of thick brown mud, with pale yellow eyes shining from their muddy heads and sharp wolfish teeth gnashing together as they moved.

"Leila, watch out!" Molly shouted, her heart thumping. This was just what she'd been dreading!

Leila gave a shout of fear and then began swimming away from the mud-monsters as fast as she could. But before she could get very far, one of the monsters snatched up a huge old trawler net that was dangling from the boat, and tossed it out through the water.

"Quick!" screamed Molly helplessly – but the net fell over Leila, trapping her inside.

Leila clawed desperately at the mesh surrounding her, but couldn't make a single tear in the netting. "Help!" she yelled. "Help me!"

Throwing back their muddy heads and laughing victoriously, the monsters hauled up Leila's thrashing body and dragged her away.

"Stop! Come back!" Molly shouted, shocked at how quickly everything was happening.

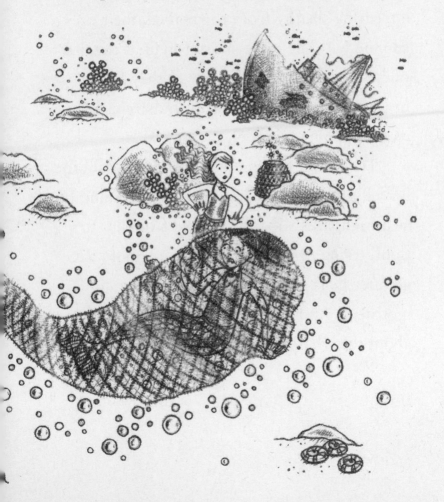

What were they going to do to Leila? And what could she, Molly, do to stop them?

Before she could think of a rescue plan, she glimpsed a movement behind her...and then gasped as she saw another group of monsters appearing silently from the seabed, their eyes shining with the same sinister light as the first ones. She gave a cry of fright as they began heading straight for her, arms outstretched, teeth snapping together.

"They want to get me as well," she said to herself under her breath, the words coming out as a frightened sob. She looked from left to right, trying to think what to do. Should she go after Leila and try to fight off the mud-monsters? And what was she going to do about the whales?

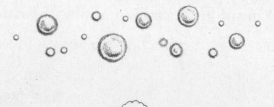

Chapter Three

Molly thought frantically. The monsters were looming ever nearer, their limbs and bodies making sickening squelching noises as they moved. She had to act fast before they dragged her away like Leila. Her silver animal charm felt warm against her skin suddenly and then an idea struck her. Previously, her charm had been able to grant her certain qualities of particular animals – it had given her the ability to swim extra-fast like a dolphin, and the ability to withstand the cold like a penguin. She'd discovered this quite by accident, but now she knew more about the charm's powers, perhaps she could use them again...

She clutched the charm between her trembling fingers. "I wish I had some armour, like a turtle's shell!" she cried. Instantly, a hologram of a turtle appeared on the shell, and she felt a tingle running all the way from the top of her spine to the tip of her tail. She knew that there would now be what she thought of as "enchanted armour", a protective force field covering her there, which meant the mud-monsters wouldn't be able to touch her.

Grabbing the lobster pot with trembling fingers, she turned her back on the monsters and swam after Leila, her heart still galloping and her adrenalin pumping.

The second group of mud-monsters tried
chasing after her and hurling rocks in her
direction, but the enchanted armour around her
was strong, and protected her from being hurt.
She was wary of getting too close to the first
group of monsters though, who were still
dragging Leila along in the net, until she

remembered another special ability the animal charm had granted her before – the power to camouflage herself like a sea horse. It had been amazing – her body had completely changed colour so that she'd blended in with her surroundings. What better way to creep closer to Leila, than to be almost invisible to others?

Holding her charm again, she said in a low voice, "I wish to camouflage myself like a sea horse!"

Instantly, she felt the force field vanish from her body just as suddenly as it had appeared. A dart of fear struck her – oh no! Had something gone wrong? Why had the force field disappeared? She felt horribly vulnerable without it.

But in the next moment, she glanced down at herself and was thrilled to see that her arms, body and tail had become the same translucent blue as the ocean around her. Even better, the lobster pot full of tiny whales was similarly camouflaged while she held it, making it impossible for the monsters to see. She could just see a faint image of a sea horse hologram on her charm before it too became camouflaged and vanished from view. So the charm's magic had worked again – but it only seemed able to grant her one animal quality at a time...

Molly swam quietly
after the first group of monsters,
carrying the heavy lobster pot as
she went. On and on trudged the
monsters, striding over the seabed in
two lines of six, like an army formation,
with Leila bundled up in the middle, still
squirming and shouting for help. Other
creatures swam out from their homes to
see what was happening but many shrank
back at the sight of the fearsome monsters.

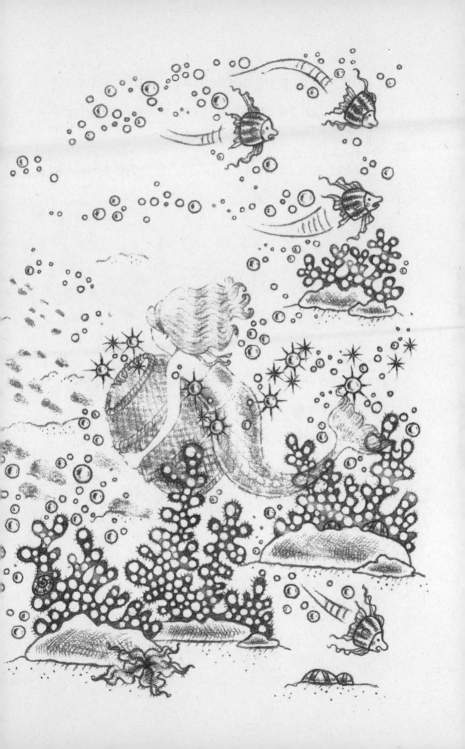

Only a group of bottlenose dolphins was brave enough to approach the monsters and scold them.

"Leave her alone! She's our friend. Untie her at once!" commanded one, waving a fin crossly at the monsters.

The monsters barely seemed to notice the dolphins were there, but went on stomping along with Leila.

The dolphin who'd spoken darted nearer still. "I said, let her go!" it cried boldly.

"Be careful!" Leila warned the brave little dolphin – but the warning came too late. The monster nearest the dolphin rounded on the animal, gnashing its sharp teeth, and the dolphins fled in fear.

After what seemed like ages, the monsters finally stopped near a rocky part of the coastline, where the water was shallower and waves crashed against a steep cliff. What would they do with Leila now? Molly wondered, hardly daring to move as she watched. Had they brought her to a secret hideout? Was the Dark Queen going to appear and work some evil magic over Leila?

She held her breath as the mud-monsters, all

working together, clambered up the rocks, dragging Leila behind them. Very slowly, so as not to be noticed, Molly broke the surface of the water so that she could watch. The sky was dark and it took a moment for Molly's eyes to adjust. Underwater she could see perfectly with her special mermaid eyes, however light or dark it was above the surface. But once her head was out of the water, she could only see as well as a human.

The monsters hauled Leila out of the water and up onto the rocks. Their eyes shone with an evil light as they clambered back into the water, then turned and headed back towards the trawler. Leila yelled and writhed on the rocks, but she was trussed up so tightly, she could hardly move. Molly's heart quickened, knowing that her friend wouldn't be able to breathe out of the water for very long. The monsters were leaving Leila there to die!

Molly had been out of the sea as a mermaid herself, when she'd helped another mermaid, Phoebe, find the missing penguins. It had been the most horrible sensation she'd ever experienced – a painful tightening of her chest as she struggled to take shallow breaths, and a paralysing dizziness as if she were going to faint at any moment. She felt sick just remembering it now. She had to get Leila down from there!

She called softly up to her friend. "Leila, can you hear me? It's Molly."

"Oh, thank goodness!" cried Leila. Her voice sounded hoarse and desperate in the cool night air. "I can hardly breathe up here – please, you've got to help me get down again!"

"I will, I promise," Molly said, although she hadn't a clue how. Her thoughts were jumbling together with panic. How could she do it? "Can you roll yourself off?" she called up.

"I'm right here, I could catch you."
There was a small shuffling
noise from up on the rocks but
then a groan of frustration. "I can
hardly move at all," Leila said
faintly. "They tied me up so tight,
I can't even twitch my tail."

Molly stared up at the cliff,
feeling helpless. The rocky ledge
on which her friend was stranded
was way out of her reach and it
would be impossible to climb up
with her slippery mermaid tail –
she'd slither straight back down.
Then she remembered the
animal charm. Was there some

animal power she could call upon that would enable her to get up to Leila more easily, perhaps, or even something that would allow her to fly?

Thinking about flying reminded her suddenly of the television footage she'd seen of whales leaping high out of the water so spectacularly, and a thought hit her. If she could do something similar, she might be able to grab Leila and somehow pull her back into the sea!

"Okay, I've had an idea," she called to Leila, feeling nervous and excited about the prospect. "I'm going to jump up out of the water and try to catch hold of you. With a bit of luck I'll pull you back in with me."

Leila didn't reply, though, just gave a moan and Molly felt a cold fear spread through her. There was no time to lose – she had to hurry up and rescue Leila before it was too late!

Chapter Four

Quickly, Molly stowed the lobster pot full of tiny whales in a nearby rock crevice. As soon as she let go of the wicker rim, the lobster pot became visible again, losing its camouflage now that she was no longer touching it.

"Charm – I need to breach like a whale," she gabbled urgently, clutching the silver disc between her fingers and hoping with all her heart that this would work.

The charm grew very hot in her hand and a whale hologram appeared on its surface. Then Molly felt a tingling sensation spread through her, rather like pins and needles. She glanced down to see that she was no longer camouflaged against the water and rocks – but nothing else was happening. *Now what?* she thought wildly. *Do I just...jump?*

She tried an experimental leap up through the water and, to her astonishment, she burst right out of the sea like the whales she'd seen, way higher than she'd expected. It felt as if she were flying, like a bird! By the light of the moon, she could just make out Leila below her, lying still on the rock, eyes closed.

The sight was so awful that Molly lost focus and completely missed Leila, smacking painfully back into the water without so much as touching her. Even worse, the mud-monsters immediately stopped and turned to see what the noise was.

They were some distance away from her now, but all the same, Molly darted behind a rock, her heart pounding, praying that they hadn't spotted her. Might they think Leila had

managed to roll herself into the water, and come to investigate?

An agonizing few seconds passed while she was convinced they were going to stomp furiously back to the coastline and catch her... but thankfully the mud-monsters turned again and continued their journey away.

Molly let out her breath in a gasp.

That had been close! She edged out from behind the rock. "Sorry, I'll try again," she called up to Leila. "Are you okay?"

There was no reply, and Molly felt tense. *Please let it not be too late to save Leila!* she thought fearfully. *Please let me get her this time!*

She leaped up once more, soaring gracefully as she rose through the air. She kept her eyes fixed on Leila's body – and this time, she just managed to grab hold of the netting wrapped around her friend as she plunged back down.

For a second, Molly panicked that Leila was going to be too heavy to pull down with her. But she was falling so fast that the force of her plummeting body meant she yanked hard on the netting – and Leila tumbled off the edge of the rocks and splashed back into the sea with Molly.

Molly cradled her friend as best she could as they hit the water. She glanced nervously in the direction the monsters had gone, but they were almost out of sight by now and hopefully far enough away that they wouldn't have heard the two mermaids falling into the water.

"Leila," she said, turning back to her friend and trying to pull the netting off her. "Leila, say something. Are you all right?"

There was a terrible moment where Leila lay lifelessly in the water, her hair swirling gently around her face with the current, her eyes still shut. "Leila, please!" Molly cried, wrenching blindly at the netting. "Can you hear me? Are you okay?"

Just as Molly was starting to feel frightened that something was badly wrong, Leila's eyelids twitched and she began to cough and splutter. Her eyes opened and she blinked, then

stared up at Molly. "What happened?" she
croaked.

"You're all right," Molly told her, relief
flooding through her. "You're all right. The
monsters are gone, and you're back in the water."

Leila coughed again, the colour returning to her cheeks. "And the whales?" she asked weakly, her eyes darting everywhere in search of them.

"They're here," Molly said, pointing to the lobster pot. "Oh, Leila," she said, the words bursting out of her, "I'm so glad you're okay. I was really starting to worry."

Leila smiled, looking better with every moment, and hugged Molly. "I must have blacked out," she said. "The last thing I remember is you saying you were going to jump out of the water to get me or something. Then…it's a blank."

"I *did* jump out of the water," Molly told her, unable to stop a surge of pride at the words. "I breached like a whale, thanks to my animal charm. It was amazing – like flying." Then she shuddered. "Those horrible monsters

– there were so many of them. We must set the whales free before they come back."

"Absolutely," Leila said, sounding more spirited now. "Come on, let's get them out."

She swam over to the lobster pot and tapped at the glassy surface that was trapping the whales inside. "Whoa, this is tough," she said, picking up a stone and knocking at the covering. "How are we going to—?" Then she stopped, and a frightened expression came over her face. "Oh, no, look!" she cried. "More monsters, Molly – heading our way!"

Chapter Five

Molly turned her head to see at least twenty of the mud-monsters advancing on them menacingly. They were armed with planks of wood, clearly torn from the old trawler, and another huge piece of netting that flowed behind them like an enormous cape. Fear and adrenalin pumped through her. Just as she'd thought they were safe, they were under attack once more!

"We've got to get away," she cried anxiously, unable to take her eyes off the fast-approaching army as they marched along the seabed, shaking their weapons threateningly at the mermaids. "And we've got to get the lobster pot to safety – that's what they're after." She thought frantically. If she and Leila didn't move fast, they would be cut off by the advancing monsters and even if they were camouflaged, it might be difficult to get away. Time to try something else. "Put your arms around my waist, Leila," she said after a moment. "And get ready for a speedy ride!"

Leila grabbed the rim of the lobster pot and did as Molly said, sliding her arms around Molly's middle and holding tight. Then Molly clutched the animal charm again. "Make me swim as fast as a dolphin!" she commanded and then...whoosh! They were away, whizzing

through the water together at a breathtaking speed. Molly's whole body was zinging with the magic from the animal charm, charged up and full of energy, as they surged away from the monsters, swerving to avoid them.

"Hold on!" Molly screamed. "And don't let go of that lobster pot!"

"Whoaaaaa!" Leila cried, clinging to Molly as she was dragged along.

Molly steered them away from the coastline, the monsters and the trawler until she and Leila

were far out into the open ocean. Only when she
was sure they were a safe distance from danger
did she come to a smooth stop. "Are you okay?"
she asked Leila, noticing that her friend's
knuckles were white from holding on so tightly.

Leila's hair was wild and tumbling all about
her face, but her eyes were shining. "That was
amazing," she said breathlessly. "What a rush!
We must have travelled so far. Well done, Molly,
that was quick thinking – and even quicker
swimming!"

Molly blushed at the praise. "This animal charm is turning out to be the most useful present ever," she told Leila. "It's saved my skin so many times already. And talking of saving things… We must get the whales out of the lobster pot now. If we can just break through this surface…"

Leila smiled. "I know an animal who can help us," she said mysteriously. "Let's see if I can call one over." She sang a few words in a strange language, and Molly turned to her curiously.

"Who are you singing to?" she couldn't help asking.

Leila pointed ahead. "Here he comes right now," she said. "Isn't he beautiful?"

Molly stared at the creature that was swimming towards them. It was a large fish, with a white belly and a grey-blue back, a crescent-shaped tail...and the most unusual face she'd ever seen. "Oh my goodness," she gasped in excitement, recognizing the creature's long, long upper jaw that stuck straight out in front of it, like a spear. "Is that a *swordfish*?"

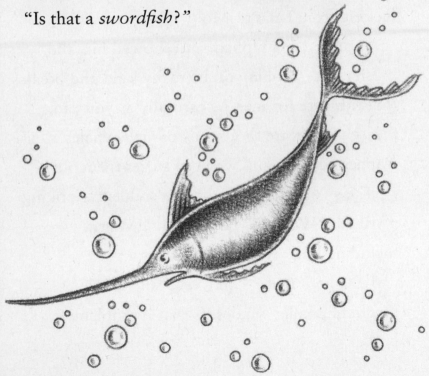

Leila nodded. "Cool, isn't he?" she said fondly. "And that sword he's got – or jaw, rather – is very sharp and strong. If anyone can pierce through to the whales, it's this guy."

The swordfish cruised towards them, his sword-like jaw cutting through the water like the prow of a ship.

"Hey there," he said, his large, round eyes flicking from Leila to Molly. "Did you call?"

"I did," Leila replied, and showed him the lobster pot. "Could you be really kind and break through here for me? As carefully as you can, please – there are thousands of little whales trapped in there and we need to get them out—"

The swordfish backed away suddenly, looking alarmed. "Whales?" he echoed. "What... Including killer whales?"

Leila hesitated. "Um...yes," she said. "Including killer whales. Is that a problem?"

The swordfish nodded, his jaw swishing up and down indignantly. "A problem? Well, yes, actually – seeing as killer whales *eat* swordfish," he said, his voice trembling. "I was just thinking this morning how relaxing and safe it has felt in the ocean lately – and now I know why. Well, you won't catch me setting those big guys free again. No way!"

Molly sympathized with the scared-looking swordfish – after all, she had been chased by a ferocious killer whale herself, in one of her first mermaid adventures. She vividly remembered just how terrifying it had been, seeing that huge, powerful black-and-white body steaming towards her! "I'm sure we can come to a deal," she told the swordfish, thinking quickly. "The whales will be so grateful to you for setting them free, I'm certain they would agree to be your friend, rather than hunt you. Don't you think, Leila?"

Leila nodded. "Absolutely," she said solemnly. "In fact, I will personally guarantee your safety from all whales, if you will just help us this time. Please? It's really important."

The swordfish looked from Leila to Molly – and then noticed Molly's animal charm. Its round eyes grew even rounder, and it bowed. "I see you are a true friend to the animals," it said respectfully, "so I, in turn, must be a true friend to you, and do what you ask me." It shivered, as if it would still rather not have

anything to do with the whales, but swam closer to the lobster pot all the same. The swordfish touched the point of its "sword" to the glassy surface and seemed to take a deep breath. "Okay," it said. "Here goes."

Molly watched the swordfish drive its strong pointed jaw against the lobster pot. There was a grinding noise as the brave swordfish pushed and pushed...and then all of a sudden, a crack appeared in the hard, glassy surface that covered the pot, and the swordfish broke right through it.

It backed off immediately and hid behind Molly while Leila pulled away the broken pieces of the glassy substance, and opened up the lobster pot. Water poured out of the pot... and so did a great gushing stream of tiny whales! As they re-entered the ocean, the whales grew bigger and bigger and *bigger*, until they were back to their usual vast sizes.

Molly gasped at the sight of the immense blue whales, fearsome killer whales and gentle humpbacks all together, like one glorious whale party everywhere she looked. "Well done," she said, hugging the swordfish, who was now shaking at the sight of so many of its enemies. "Oh, well done. That was really brave of you. Thank you!"

Leila meanwhile was whooping with joy and swimming from whale to whale, kissing them and stroking them happily. Then she remembered the courageous swordfish and clapped her hands together. "It's wonderful to see you safe and healthy again," she said, holding the silvery whale charm on her necklace as she spoke. It fizzed with bright red magic sparkles which spread out through the water in glittering trails, as if carrying her message to every whale. "Just one thing before you all swim away," she called, then beckoned to the swordfish, who swam timidly towards her. "This guy just set you free from where you were imprisoned and I now declare him a friend to all whales. Nobody is allowed to eat him, all right?"

The whales bowed their mighty heads respectfully in the direction of the swordfish, and a few even sang to him in gratitude.

"Good job," Leila told the swordfish, who looked relieved and now rather proud of himself. "You're a friend to mermaids, too. Thanks again."

"Pleasure," the swordfish said, bowing his long jaw bashfully. "Glad I could help."

Leila watched him swim quickly away, then turned back to the whales. "I'll come and check on you all individually as soon as I can," she told them. "But now, you really should swim to your homes, or set off on your migration routes. Let's get back to normal as quickly as possible."

Far from swimming happily away, though, the whales seemed confused about where to go. Some were even bumping into one another as they moved around, as if they couldn't see properly.

"Are they all right?" Molly asked Leila. "Why aren't they going anywhere?"

Leila bit her lip, her face suddenly clouded with worry. "They don't seem to have any sense of direction," she said uneasily. "I don't think their echolocation skills can be working properly." She winced as she saw a large sperm whale bump clumsily into a rock on the seabed. "Oh, no," she said. "This is a disaster!"

Chapter Six

"Echolocation – isn't that how dolphins find their way around too?" Molly asked, trying to remember what she'd learned about it as part of her school project.

Leila nodded, still watching the whales anxiously. "Yes," she replied. "They send out high-pitched sounds that bounce off nearby objects and return to the whale. The whale can tell by the sounds what shape and size the object is, and how far away it is. So they use it not only to find out where they are, but also to hunt food. Without their echolocation, they'll get lost and may even end up beached and stranded – it could be really dangerous. And it's going to be difficult for lots of them to find food now too."

Molly didn't like the sound of this at all. She hated seeing the big friendly giants of the ocean so confused. "The Dark Queen must have taken this power from them," she realized, remembering how Carlotta had stripped the other creatures of their special abilities too. "Oh, we've got to get it back – they seem really lost without it."

Leila nodded. "It's such a basic tool for them – they use it constantly," she said. "We *must* find Carlotta and defeat her, so that we can get it back for them. Although she is going to be absolutely formidable, now that she has taken all the powers for herself…"

Molly shivered. She'd seen Carlotta once before and had found her a terrifyingly evil and dangerous enemy. Beating her was going to be harder than ever, but of course Leila was right – the mermaids *had* to defeat her. There was simply no other option. "There are just the octopuses left to find now," she said, thinking aloud. "And—"

But before she could finish speaking, she caught sight of a familiar light shining through the water. Dawn was breaking, and it was time to return to her own world. She just managed to hug Leila before she felt the usual pulling sensation, as if she were being reeled in from the ocean like a fish on a line. "Take care," she shouted quickly. "I'll be back soon, hopefully and…"

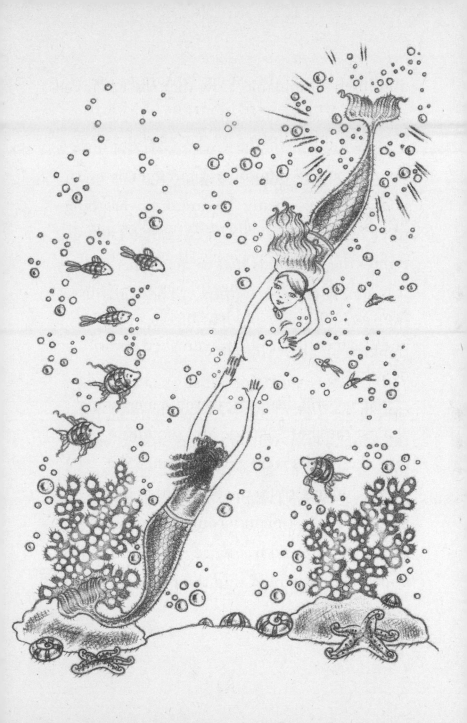

With a great whooshing sensation, the mermaid world blurred in front of Molly's eyes, and then all she saw was darkness.

"I'll be back soon," she murmured fitfully – and then, opening her eyes, she realized she was in bed, and home again. She was a girl now, with pyjama-clad legs under the duvet, and her mermaid tail had vanished...until next time.

She lay still, listening to the sea crashing against the shore outside and wondering how the whales were getting along. She hated thinking of them so bewildered and lost – it was just plain wrong. But at least they were safe and free once more, and hopefully they would find their way home, with Leila's help.

"Just the octopuses left to find now," she murmured to herself. And then, with a bit of luck, she, the mermaids and their animal friends could come up with a plan to defeat Carlotta once and for all...

She smiled to herself suddenly as she heard her dad belting out "Hark! the Herald Angels Sing" downstairs. He wasn't quite as good a singer as the whales, it had to be said, but the sound gave her a lovely Christmassy feeling. Goodness, life was exciting these days!

The End

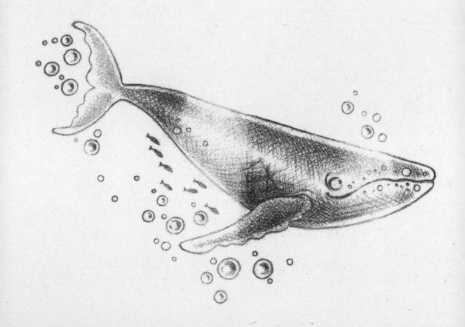

Read on for a sneak preview of Molly's next magical underwater adventure...

The Dark Queen's Revenge

That night, after Molly had said goodnight to her parents and Gran, she made sure her special necklace was in its usual place, on her bedside table. The pale piece of conch shell gleamed in the darkness and she reached out to touch it, and the silver animal charm, with her fingertips. "Please let the magic work tonight," she whispered. She didn't become a mermaid every night, unfortunately, however much she would have liked to. She knew that she had to wait for the magic to happen all on its own.

Shutting her eyes, she rolled over, pulling the covers right up around her neck. It was cold that night, and she could feel the freezing sea air whispering through her draughty bedroom windows. She tossed and turned for a while, trying to get comfortable, and then, just as she was starting to think she was never going to fall asleep, she sensed a sudden brightness in the room, even through her closed eyes, and opened them at once.

Yes! The conch shell on her necklace was shining through the darkness, with pink sparkly magic streaming out from it. That only meant one thing…she was about to have a mermaid adventure!

She shut her eyes again hurriedly and the magic took hold in the very next second.

As always, Molly felt as if she were falling very fast and very far, as if a giant hand had picked her up and then dropped her. Then a warm, tingly feeling spread throughout her body and she heard gentle splashing sounds. Now she could feel the weightlessness of being in water, and opened her eyes immediately to see that once again, she was a mermaid, with her own glittering green tail. Hooray!

Molly was in a coral reef this time, and she gazed around in delight at all the different coloured fish and other creatures swimming past her. There were gorgeous striped clown fish whizzing by in a blur of orange, and a spiny puffer fish cruising sedately along with a haughty expression on its face. Elsewhere, there were crabs scuttling across the seabed, green and blue plants rippling like beckoning fingers... Oh, and there was another mermaid swimming towards her, smiling and waving!

Molly recognized Iona at once – she had met her along with all the other Animal-Keeper mermaids in Queen Luna's palace courtyard when the animals had first gone missing. Iona had long brown hair, tied up in a ponytail and pale skin dotted with freckles. She had a wide smile and beautiful violet eyes, and a silver octopus charm which dangled from a chain around her neck.

"Hello there," Molly said as she approached. "Nice to see you again! Any news on the octopuses?"

"Hi," Iona replied. "I don't have any definite news, although I've come here to investigate something that a couple of jellyfish told me about. There's a 'magic walking cowrie shell' in this reef apparently, which sounds very unusual. I couldn't help wondering if it had something to do with the missing octopuses. Want to help me check it out?"

"A magic walking cowrie shell?" Molly repeated in surprise. "That does sound weird. Where is it supposed to be?"

"Near the seaweed jungle at the edge of the reef, they said," Iona replied. "It's this way. Follow me."

To find out what happens next, read

The Secret Mermaid

The Dark Queen's Revenge

To find out more
about Molly and all her
mermaid friends, and have
some magical ocean fun,
check out
www.thesecretmermaid.co.uk

Collect all of Molly's magical mermaid adventures

Enchanted Shell ⊙ 9780746096154

Molly is transported to the Undersea Kingdom for the first time, where she discovers she is the secret mermaid!

Seaside Adventure ⊙ 9780746096161

To help Ella recover her piece of the magical conch, Molly must find a way to trap an angry killer whale.

Underwater Magic ⊙ 9780746096178

Can Molly find some pirate treasure to win back Delphi's shell from a grumpy sea urchin?

Reef Rescue ⊙ 9780746096192

Molly must help Coral find her shell to restore the ocean reefs, but a swarm of jellyfish stands in their way...

Deep Trouble ⊙ 9780746096185

Pearl's conch piece is trapped in an undersea volcano and guarded by sea snakes. How can she and Molly release it?

Return of the Dark Queen ⊙ 9780746096208

Molly must save Shivana from an Arctic prison before the Shell-Keeper mermaids can finally face the Dark Queen and complete the magical conch.

Seahorse SOS ⊚ 9781409506324

There's more trouble in the Undersea Kingdom and Molly joins in the search for the missing seahorses.

Dolphin Danger ⊚ 9781409506331

Molly and Aisha can hear faint calls for help but the dolphins are nowhere to be seen. Where can they be?

Penguin Peril ⊚ 9781409506348

Could the Dark Queen be behind the mysterious disappearance of the penguins from the icy seas?

Turtle Trouble ⊚ 9781409506355

There are some scary monsters lurking in the coral reef and they're guarding the turtles Molly has come to set free!

Whale Rescue ⊚ 9781409506393

Molly must not only save the trapped whales but also her mermaid friend, Leila.

The Dark Queen's Revenge ⊚ 9781409506409

The Dark Queen is back and she wants to rule the Undersea Kingdom with her bad magic. Can Molly put an end to her vile plans?

For more enchanting adventures
log on to
www.fiction.usborne.com